Dear Parents and Educators,

Welcome to Penguin Young Readers! As parents and educators, you know that each child develops at his or her own pace—in terms of speech, critical thinking, and, of course, reading. Penguin Young Readers recognizes this fact. As a result, each Penguin Young Readers book is assigned a traditional easy-to-read level (1–4) as well as a Guided Reading Level (A–P). Both of these systems will help you choose the right book for your child. Please refer to the back of each book for specific leveling information. Penguin Young Readers features esteemed authors and illustrators, stories about favorite characters, fascinating nonfiction, and more!

Fox Be Nimble	LEVEL **3**
	GUIDED READING LEVEL **J**

This book is perfect for a **Transitional Reader** who:
- can read multisyllable and compound words;
- can read words with prefixes and suffixes;
- is able to identify story elements (beginning, middle, end, plot, setting, characters, problem, solution); and
- can understand different points of view.

Here are some **activities** you can do during and after reading this book:
- Character Traits: Fox is the main character in these stories. Come up with a list of words to describe him.
- Make Connections: Put yourself in Fox's place. If you were Fox, would you agree to babysit for your neighbor's kids? Would you make a big fuss over a small injury? How would you feel about participating in the big parade?

Remember, sharing the love of reading with a child is the best gift you can give!

—Bonnie Bader, EdM, and Katie Carella, EdM
    Penguin Young Readers program

*Penguin Young Readers are leveled by independent reviewers applying the standards developed by Irene Fountas and Gay Su Pinnell in *Matching Books to Readers: Using Leveled Books in Guided Reading*, Heinemann, 1999.

For Olivia, Nicholas, Manton, and
Thacher Hurd—JM

Penguin Young Readers
Published by the Penguin Group
Penguin Group (USA) Inc., 375 Hudson Street, New York, New York 10014, USA
Penguin Group (Canada), 90 Eglinton Avenue East, Suite 700, Toronto, Ontario M4P 2Y3,
Canada (a division of Pearson Penguin Canada Inc.)
Penguin Books Ltd., 80 Strand, London WC2R 0RL, England
Penguin Group Ireland, 25 St. Stephen's Green, Dublin 2, Ireland (a division of Penguin Books Ltd.)
Penguin Group (Australia), 250 Camberwell Road, Camberwell, Victoria 3124, Australia
(a division of Pearson Australia Group Pty. Ltd.)
Penguin Books India Pvt. Ltd., 11 Community Centre, Panchsheel Park, New Delhi—110 017, India
Penguin Group (NZ), 67 Apollo Drive, Rosedale, Auckland 0632, New Zealand
(a division of Pearson New Zealand Ltd.)
Penguin Books (South Africa) (Pty.) Ltd., 24 Sturdee Avenue, Rosebank,
Johannesburg 2196, South Africa

Penguin Books Ltd., Registered Offices: 80 Strand, London WC2R 0RL, England

Text and illustrations copyright © 1990 by James Marshall. All rights reserved. First published in 1990
by Dial Books for Young Readers and in 1994 by Puffin Books, imprints of Penguin Group (USA) Inc.
Published in 2011 by Penguin Young Readers, an imprint of Penguin Group (USA) Inc.,
345 Hudson Street, New York, New York 10014. Manufactured in China.

The Library of Congress has cataloged the Dial edition
under the following Control Number: 89007933

ISBN 978-0-14-036842-0   10

PENGUIN YOUNG READERS

LEVEL

3

TRANSITIONAL READER

FOX BE NIMBLE

by James Marshall

Penguin Young Readers
An Imprint of Penguin Group (USA) Inc.

Contents

FOX THE FAMOUS

Fox's mom was on the phone.

"Fox would *love* to help,"
said Mom.

"I'll send him right over."

"I won't do it," said Fox.

"Whatever it is.

I'm playing rock star."

"Mrs. Ling across the street needs you to sit with her kids," said Mom.

"Why don't *you* do it?" said Fox.

"This is my quiet time," said Mom. "Now hurry up."

"No," said Fox.

"And that is that."

"Oh really?" said Mom.

And Fox went across the street.

"How nice of you, Fox,"

said Mrs. Ling.

"Mom made me,"

said Fox.

Mrs. Ling got into her car.

"I do hope they behave," she said.

"I can handle them," said Fox.

"They're just kids."

Mrs. Ling drove off.

"Hot dog!" yelled the Ling kids.

And they went wild.

"Stop that!" cried Fox.

"Come down from there!" cried Fox.

"Quit it!" cried Fox.

"I don't have time for this!"

But the Ling kids would not quit.

They did just what they wanted.

Fox had to get tough.

"I'll tell your mom!" he said.

The Ling kids got very still.

"We'll be good," they said.

"Why don't you go play
in the backyard?" said Fox.

The kids liked that idea.

"May we play with our new balloons?"
they said.

"I don't see why not,"
said Fox.

Fox went back to playing rock star.

"The girls will love this," he said.

Suddenly he had an odd feeling.

The Ling kids were up to something.

Fox ran into the backyard.

"Come back here this minute!"

he cried.

"Bye-bye!" the Ling kids called out.

"Oh, no!" cried Fox.

"Their mom will *kill* me!

I'll have to catch them!"

He climbed the fence.

And he fell right into some mud,

tore his brand-new blue jeans,

tripped and stubbed his toe,

and ran smack into Mrs. O'Hara.

Then Fox got a bright idea.

He climbed up

to a very high place.

"I'll grab them when they float by,"

he said.

He tried not to look down.

Fox didn't like high places.

But the wind carried the Ling kids
right back home.

"What have you little darlings
been up to?" said Mrs. Ling.
"And just *what* have you done
with poor Fox?"

That night Fox's mom
turned on the TV.
"A fox was rescued from a high
place today," said the newscaster.
"Why that's *you*, Fox!" said Mom.
"Fox is famous!" cried little Louise.
"Oh, quit it!" said Fox.

FOX THE BRAVE

Fox stepped on one of his skates
and went flying.

"Who left *that* there?" he cried.

And he landed with a bang.

Mom and Louise came running.

"I'm dying!" cried Fox.

"It's only a scratch," said Mom.

"Nothing to worry about."

"I can't look at all the blood!"
cried Fox.

"There's no blood," said Mom.

"Don't leave me!" cried Fox.

Mom and Louise put Fox to bed.

"Call Doctor Ed," said Fox.

"Before it's too late."

"Really, Fox," said Mom.

"You're making *such* a fuss."

Louise called Doctor Ed to come over.

Then she stepped on Fox's other skate,

bounced down the stairs,

flew right out the front door,

and ran smack into Mrs. O'Hara.

"Poor Louise must hurt all over,"

said Doctor Ed.

But Louise didn't cry.

She didn't complain.

Not even a peep.

"Very brave," said Doctor Ed.

"Very brave."

"Louise is tough," said Mom.

"Now then," said Doctor Ed.

"What's the matter with Fox?"

"Oh, it's just a scratch," said Fox.

"I don't like to make a fuss."

Mom didn't say a word.

FOX
ON
PARADE

"Fox is showing off!"

said Dexter.

"Quit it, Fox," said Mr. Sharp.

"We don't have time for this.

The big parade is next week."

And the band played on.

"Fox is showing off again!"

said Carmen.

"That does it!" said Mr. Sharp.

Fox was told to leave the band room. "Come back when you have changed your ways," said Mr. Sharp. "But I *like* to show off," said Fox.

Fox sat in the school yard by himself.

"There are some things
you just *can't* change," he said.

"Look out! Look out!"
cried a voice.

Fox almost got hit.

"Oh, dear!" cried his friend Raisin.

"I'm *so* clumsy!"

"You should be more careful!"
said Fox crossly.

"I'm sorry," said Raisin.

"I'm just not good at this."

"It looks easy to me," said Fox.

"Oh really?" said Raisin.

"Then *you* try it."

Fox gave the baton a twirl.

And he dropped it on his toe.

"Ouch!" he yelled.

"This is harder than it looks."

But soon he got the hang of it

and he got better and better.

Raisin couldn't believe her eyes.

"Wow!" said Dexter.

"Will you look at *that*!"

"Fox," said Mr. Sharp.

"May I speak to you a moment?"

"What now?" said Fox.

On the day of the big parade